Crumpet Court Chronicles

Dakota McElhinny

Tale I:
Of Wolf and Magic

Chapter I

The New Hound

He bustled along the cobblestone walkway, pulling his briefcase closer to his hip. The fog hung like a toxic vapor—it was London after all. His eyes shot about, he was unsure of what to expect, but not too far away it stood, *The Red Lion Pub.*

He entered the pub, stomping the muck off his boots before walking any further—he was a neat fellow.

"Alistair, wonderful to see you! What'll it be?" the pub-keeper asked.

"Lager, Ernie," he replied, making his way to the counter.

"All right, it'll be a moment."

Alistair looked over the pub, filled with peculiar people, but none more peculiar than Mr. Wharton. "I'll be at my spot, Ernie, bring it when you can."

"I will."

Alistair made his way to a small booth. Old Mr. Wharton sat on one side, his gunmetal-blue eyes stared out the window, and he wore a black vest with silky purple fringes. "It's good to see you, Victor," Alistair said, placing himself and his briefcase in the free seat.

"I'm glad you could make it," Victor replied, though his line of vision remained on the outside world.

"What do you have for me?"

"The usual." A dry smirk slid across his lips, "a dull, boring *story* for the newspaper."

Alistair grinned. "I assumed as much, when you summoned."

"Did you?"

"Of course, but where's Arthur?"

"At home, I don't need him for this one."

"But he documents all your fun times."

"Not in a glowing manner, as you," Victor replied. He finally turned his gaze to Alistair. "Tell me, will you be putting our adventure in?"

"Of course, the usual. Everyone wants a good read, Victor, you of all know that."

"No, everyone wants an embellished story."

"And every good story needs a little embellishment."

Victor's gaze returned to the cold streets. "And will you be painting well?"

"Painting what, exactly?"

"Me, Alistair, I read your story on our good friend, Van Hoth, last week, and it could have used more—what's the right word?"

"Embellishment?"

Victor grinned and nodded his head. "Please, paint me well."

"I give the people what they want, Victor, nothing more and nothing less."

"Ah, spoken like a true journalist."

"Victor, play nice."

"Always, dear Alistair, always."

Ernie arrived at the table, placing a lager down for Alistair and another scotch for Victor. After a thankful nod, Alistair sipped his drink, and his eyes turned to the streets. "What are we hunting, Victor?"

That devilish grin returned, again. "Something that will make Arthur's *Hound* look like child's play."

"I don't follow."

"How's your studies in lycanthropy?"

"I'm not familiar with the field, but lycan is an interchangeable word for wolf."

"Not a wolf. Lycanthropy is the scientific study of the werewolf."

"A werewolf?"

"Yes, and it's been the most thrilling adventure since retirement."

"Victor, are you mad? Why can't you hunt a normal monster?"

"Monsters are boring. I've been hunting them all my life, and I put them all in prison."

"Then, what about Mary's problem?"

Victor rolled his eyes. "I knew it would come to this."

"Victor, I spoke with her recently, and she is close to finding him. You need to help her."

"I don't and I won't."

"She is your friend."

Victor gave a puzzled look. "Are people actually friends with their doctors? Besides, I have Arthur, and I've not spoken with Mary in some time."

"If you would answer her telegrams, then you would be on speaking terms."

Victor's nose cringed. "Ah, the telegrams—they make fine firewood replacements, you know."

"Victor, he is a threat."

"Mary created him, and she can deal with him. I don't want a monster, I want a beast, and I have chosen the werewolf."

"Victor—"

"Listen to me, Alistair, I'm allowing you and the lovely *Crumpet* to accompany me, but in return, I do not want to hear about Mary," Victor replied, squinting hard to see through the fog outside. "And I also want you to paint me well."

"All right, all right, whatever you say, Victor."

"Good, now get your pen and pad ready."

"Where?" Alistair asked, looking outside.

"Look away!" Victor snapped. "We cannot both gawk. When I look away, you may take a glance."

Victor's head turned to his scotch, and Alistair stole a quick peek. "The bum?" he asked, confused with no one else in sight.

"Alistair, use your eyes," Victor urged. "Red skin, raven-black hair. He is a native from America. Their cultures are rich with myths and legends of werewolves and night creatures." Victor smiled, staring. "Oh, it's perfect! The hunter is hiding in the open, searching for his prey."

"What's our plan?"

"Take the bait and set our own trap. This is the last full moon, until next month," Victor whispered, throwing his jacket on hurriedly. "If we are successful tonight, then you can assist Mary and catch her *story* next week."

Alistair smirked at the quip. "And if we fail, then I suppose we will meet at next month's first full moon."

"Oh, Alistair, you cut me deep."

The two men left their money on the table, thanked Ernie for the fine drinks, and set off. The fog had thickened, but the two could distinctly see Victor's fellow, lurking and stalking after them.

"What now, Victor? He is following."

"It needs to feed, and what better prey than an old man and a wordsmith."

"How can he tell?"

"You are still holding the pen, Alistair."

Alistair shoved the pen into his pocket. "Where are we going?"

"The docks, I have a fancy for some fishing."

"What will we do there?"

"What do you do when you fish? You wait."

Their paces quickened through the streets, knowing their hunter was not far behind. Victor's eyes glanced to his pocket watch. It was ten minutes until the full moon's midnight, and then the fun would begin. Meanwhile, Alistair toyed with words in his mind for his story, in the *Crumpet.*

Oh, the paradox of it all. Crumpets were meant to be sweet, and the *Crumpet Court Chronicles* certainly delivered on those savory stories; but there was nothing sweet about Alistair's tales, unless the reader fancied suspense and horror. In truth, if it had not been for Alistair being a Crumpet, he would have never found any page time with his stories.

The young writer snapped from his word-crafting, as he realized the docks were coming into sight. Victor looked down to his pocket watch. Five minutes until midnight, five minutes to show time.

Chapter II

The Dance Begins

The air was cooler down at the docks, and there was a salty breeze blowing about. Victor swept around the closest rental cabin, and Alistair was right behind him. The old detective took out a small pistol, loading it.

"What is that?" Alistair asked, finding the bullet odd.

"A tranquilizer."

"What will it do?"

"Hopefully, put our friend to sleep."

"Hopefully? You mean, you are not certain?"

Victor shrugged. "I've never faced a werewolf, and this is all we have."

"Did you not come up with any plan?"

"Where is it?"

Alistair turned around, peering through the fog. "I don't see him, anywhere. Victor, are you sure you were right?" Alistair turned to his friend, but Mr. Wharton had completely vanished.

Alistair looked back, glancing at the fog. "Victor? Victor? Confound it, where have you run off to?"

Alistair began walking slowly, his back to the rental cabin. Had he known, he would be dancing with a werewolf, he would have bought a pistol. Without one, he felt naked.

As Alistair crept around the backside of the cabin, he

whipped his head back, quite sure he heard the sound of scampering. Nothing. Nothing but the thick fog, surrounded by a sea of black night, and a full moon providing little comfort.

"Victor?" He reached into his pocket, pulling out his pen and uncapping it. If the werewolf came upon him, he would not fall without a scuffle. "Victor?"

No voice replied to dear Mr. Alistair, only a low growl. The werewolf was indeed near, just as he had suspected, but where? Alistair froze, his back seemed glued to the cabin, and his hand ready to plunge the pen.

Something grabbed him, and Alistair jumped. "*Shhh,* don't move!" It was only Victor, and he was pulling for Alistair to follow him.

The young writer's legs may have been like the queen's jelly, but he moved quickly and followed Victor. The old detective took them both closer to the docks, and into one of the smaller fishing schooners.

"Where did you run off to?"

"Here, why did you stay behind?"

"Victor," Alistair whispered, flustered, "I'm not armed; I have to stay with you."

Victor could not hold back a smile. "Isn't the pen mightier than the sword?"

"Ha-ha," Alistair replied, dryly, "I'll show you how mighty the pen can be, once this hits the *Crumpet.*"

"Take this," Victor said, handing over the pistol.

Alistair looked at it, frightfully. "Victor, I disapprove of firearms, you know this. Besides, what will you use?"

"I suggest, you become friends with that pistol, my dear Alistair, since it is the only thing that may save your life tonight," Victor replied, reaching down and moving some ropes aside. "As for myself, I will be using this." The old detective pulled up a slim rifle, with a long, narrow barrel and a scope.

"You were prepared for this?"

Victor smirked. "You believed I wasn't?"

Alistair gave a deep exhale. He had assumed everything was happening by chance, but to know Victor had a plan gave him some relief.

Victor knelt, placing the barrel on the boat's side, and he peered through the scope. "Don't talk, Alistair."

"What are you doing?"

"I said, don't talk."

Alistair struggled to look through the fog. He did not see any werewolf, so he was unsure of what Victor was aiming at or intending to shoot. He listened quietly, Victor's breathes were becoming less and shallower. Then, it happened. *Bang!*

"Hurry, Alistair!" Victor exclaimed, jumping up and running off.

Alistair took off, following after the old detective. He could hear Victor's feet patter through a puddle *splash, splash,* then he could hear Victor bolting down the next dock *thud, thud.*

"Get it Alistair!"

Alistair heard an irritated snarling. Something had jumped from Victor's dock, back to the one Alistair was about to pass. He stopped at the top and aimed the pistol. Everything was silent.

"Shoot, Alistair, shoot!"

Alistair opened his mouth to reply, *at what*, but then, it came barreling down the dock. It was large with grayish white fur and sickly yellow eyes. Alistair froze, dropping his pistol. The creature lunged at him, but a shot rang out. What happened Alistair could not say, but he found himself lying on his back, and the creature—surely, Victor's werewolf—had vanished.

"What happened, Alistair? You had it."

"Victor, did you see it?"

"Yes, I saw it, but I did not lose my wits."

"I'll lose my wits again, if I must lay eyes on that beast."

"Well, if you—and your readers—would like to know the ending of our story, then I'm afraid, I will have to call on you again."

Alistair's heart seemed to skip a beat. He knew, with their failure to catch the werewolf, Victor would continue his hunt. "Where will we go now?"

"Home," Victor replied, "hopefully, to a warm drink."

"Then, you do not intend to chase it tonight?"

"My dear Alistair, London is a large city, and I'm not young enough to go traipsing about, chasing it. Besides, I do not know where its lair is."

Alistair let out a rough exhale, as he grabbed the pistol beside him, and rose to his feet. He looked down at the weapon, wondering what to do with it. "May I keep this for tonight?"

"Of course," Victor replied, "fancy a drink at my place?"

Alistair shook his head. "No, I need to write all this out and have it ready for the *Crumpet*, in the morning."

Chapter III

Father Knows Best

"Alistair, come in here!"

Alistair rubbed his groggy eyes, and clutched the side of his head, as it rang badly. The empty scotch bottle told him enough.

"Alistair, now!"

Young Mr. Crumpet placed his hands on his desk and rose to his feet, slightly staggering. He had spent another night at the office. The sun was up, only worsening how he felt. He stumbled from his desk, though, and into the next room.

"Ah, good morning, Alistair, how are you?"

Alistair adjusted his eyes and smiled. "I'm well, father, and you?"

Old man Crumpet gave a wide grin. "I am well, I am well," he replied, easing his heavy frame back in his chair. "Your mother made me fried bacon, and I had chives and cheese on my bagel. Always a beautiful delicacy."

"Never a wrong choice."

"Indeed," old man Crumpet replied, with a hearty laugh, "then, I came to work, and I read your sister's story on Alexander Bullworth's money laundering scheme. Quite delicious—front page worthy for sure."

Alistair nodded. "I'm sure she makes you proud."

"Oh, she does," old man Crumpet said, as his face turned from jovial to stern, "and then, Alistair, I read your story." He looked down at the paper in front of him and tossed it to the forefront of his desk. "What is this?"

Alistair shrugged. "Last week concluded my *German Ghoul Lose in London* series, and I wanted to follow it up with a fierce predator."

Old man Crumpet shook his head. "Alistair, you're a Crumpet, and we Crumpets are reporters. The people want the sweet, juicy stories, and we cannot give them that, if you are day-dreaming the next London terror." Mr. Crumpet ran his porky finger over his thick, wooly mustache. "How will we remedy this?"

"There is nothing to remedy, father. Ainsley collects your front-page news, and I entertain our readers in the back column."

"Alistair, Alistair, Alistair," old man Crumpet sighed. "I need news, son, and I cannot keep you on, if this is what you are going to give me."

Alistair's face sunk. "Father, you can't take the *Crumpet* from me. It's all I have."

"What am I to do?"

"No one, besides a Crumpet, has ever been published in the *Crumpet Court Chronicles*."

"I know that, Alistair, but your stories are giving me no choice but to change that."

"If that changes, I'll be leaving," a soft, firm voice said, from behind Alistair. He turned around, happy to find Ainsley in the doorway. "You hear me, father? If Alistair is tossed, then I'll be heading out as well."

"Oh, Ainsley. Your brother is not living up to the Crumpet name, or the *Crumpet's* standards."

She stepped into the room, standing by Alistair's side, and her muddy eyes met her father's aged hazel. "The *Crumpet's* or yours?"

Old man Crumpet rose to his feet, wagging his porky finger at her. "You are out of line, Ainsley."

"Our readers enjoy the scoops I break, but they also love Alistair's stories."

Old man Crumpet looked to Alistair. "This is all your doing, I know it. You've turned her against me."

"Oh, father," Ainsley said.

"No, I know best," he replied, heatedly, "but if keeping Alistair and his stories, keeps you, then so be it. But, Alistair, I want more from you, son."

"I will try, father."

Old man Crumpet sat his heavy frame down. "All right, get back to work, both of you."

Ainsley turned and gave Alistair a hard look, while Alistair returned a weak smile. They both walked out, with him closing the door.

"What did you write about this time?"

Alistair placed his hands against his temples, relieving the pain. "Um," he replied, followed by a deep exhale. "A werewolf."

"A werewolf?" He nodded at her. "Alistair, I cannot keep doing this."

"I know," he replied, "I did not ask you to intervene, and I never do."

"Alistair, this is father's dream. Him running the *Crumpet* and us writing for it. Would it hurt to do your job?"

"I do."

"No, Alistair, you write stories, and our readers enjoy them, but father doesn't. He wants us to take this serious."

"Ainsley, I turn in a story on time, every time."

"Alistair," she said with a sigh, as a sneaky smirk painted her face.

"Wait." He looked at her, knowing something had happened. "What is it?"

She gave a giddy smile. "I was offered the job at *Skyline*."

Alistair's eyes widened. "You took it?"

"I have not decided yet," she replied, "but this is why you need to be on good terms with father. I may not always be here, to save you."

Alistair nodded his head, as he sat back down at his desk. "You're right, I'll try to do better. But about you, you are taking the job at *Skyline*, yes?"

"I've not decided yet, and I don't know how father would take it, knowing his only daughter accepted an offer to the towering

Skyline, while his *Crumpet* loses flavor."

Alistair smiled. "I would still be here."

"Writing your stories, until he sacked you."

Alistair looked at her, full of admiration. "You deserve that job, Ainsley. You deserve to be happy."

"Who said I was not happy here, at the *Crumpet?*"

Alistair smirked. "Knowing your boss, I know you're not."

Ainsley laughed at his quip. "Maybe you should drop the stories, Alistair, and start a comedy page."

"Ah, but obviously, you have the jokes, dear sister."

She turned to her desk, while he began perusing the mail on his desk, and he smiled finding a note from Mary.

Alistair,

Please find this as a request for your presence today at 4 for tea. If you need further incentive, I have a story. My home as always.

Warm wishes, Mary

Ainsley picked up her briefcase, rummaging through the contents. "I have an interview with several of Bullworth's former employees. I will be out the rest of the day, so stay out of trouble with father, and go find a story."

Alistair smiled. "Yes, of course, I will find a story, but only because father knows best."

Chapter IV

Mary's Monster

Clop, clop, clop, clop. The great Clydesdales trotted down the cobblestone walkways. Alistair looked out from the buggy, watching all of London pass him.

Big gray buildings sat lined in a row, flat with sadness. In the distance, black smoke billowed upwards, from the monstrous factories. Factories. The downfall of man, if you asked Alistair. There was no joy in them, just a monotonous, mundane feel. *Puff, puff,* the black smokes rose higher.

"Oh, the irony of it all," Alistair whispered, though he meant it to be a thought.

"The irony of what, sir?" the buggy driver asked.

Alistair looked to him. He had not truly paid attention to the driver before. He was a thin fellow, with straggly gray hair and a beard, and he was missing three fingers on his left hand. "The factories," young Mr. Crumpet replied, "men and women slave away in them, fighting for petty wages, and all the while, the black smoke puffs on."

The buggy driver gave a nod. "Too true, sir, but we must do what we can to put food on the table."

"Yes, I suppose," Alistair said, pitying those slaving souls. "But, isn't that man's fate? Are we all not a short *puff*?"

"Ah, good sir, you speak from the Book of James," the buggy

driver replied. *"For what is your life? It is even a vapour, that appeareth for a little time, and then vanisheth away."*

For a moment, Alistair pondered the words. He did not consider himself a Biblical fellow, but the good Word held truth. "Yes, that is exactly it. *Puff,* and those poor people are gone; others will replace them until *puff,* they are gone, too; and they will be replaced."

"As you said, sir, that's man's fate. Remember the poet's words: *O, dear fate! How you are cruel and unkind; Taking away free-will and making pathways pre-designed."*

"You believe that?"

"Believe what, sir?"

"That everyone has a fate, and life is pre-destined."

The buggy driver mused for a moment. "Fate is a tricky word. Everyone has a fate to die. Sometimes we make decisions, locking in certain fates. As for pre-destination, no, I don't. I believe the good Word, when it tells us man has a choice." He raised his bad hand up. "Of course, I stand by life can be cruel and unkind. Lost them during the war."

"What happened?"

"Rifle barrel exploded in my hands." The buggy driver chuckled. "Funny enough, if it weren't for this, I'd probably be there, in those factories."

Alistair looked back to the factories. The black smoke billowed ever-on. Then he realized, the buggy was slowing to a stop, and Mary's house sat on the left.

He climbed out of the buggy and turned to the driver. "It was a delight to speak with you, Mr.—"

"Snipes."

"Mr. Snipes," Alistair said, reaching up and shaking the buggy driver's hand.

"As you, Mr. Crumpet," Mr. Snipes replied, and he started his buggy down the street, looking for his next passenger.

Alistair walked pass the black iron fence, up to the red door, and he knocked. He glanced down at the stone creature beside him. Most people had a lion sitting, decorating the front of their home, but not Mary. No, she had to display a gargoyle. This only seemed fitting to Alistair, though, as Mary was far from being normal.

The door opened. "Yes?" a new butler—or at least new to Alistair—asked.

"Mr. Crumpet," Alistair said, handing over his invitation, "here for tea."

The butler took the invitation, examining it. "Follow me."

He led Alistair into Mary's home. Alistair had only been to her home on a handful of occasions. Her black-and-white checkered floors were always well polished, and as they passed the large staircase, Alistair was ushered into the parlor room. Its walls were covered in portraits of famous people and paintings of far-off lands and seas. Alistair always admired them.

"Alistair, it has been far too long," a loving voice said,

greeting him with a kiss on the cheek.

"Mary," he replied, smiling. "How have you been?"

"Better, I assure you, but let's sit and have our tea before indulging into life and its horrors."

The two sat on velvety plush chairs. Alistair stared at the painting to his left, one of a beautiful beach with white sands and a glittering sapphire sea.

"You like?" she asked him.

"Of course."

"It is of some beach, located in the Caribbean Sea, south of the States."

"Have you been?"

Mary laughed, though it sounded fake and forced. "No, when would I find the time?" she asked. "Sugar, dear?"

"Yes, please."

"One lump, or two?"

"One, please."

She handed him a teacup, and he took a sip. "Oh, Mary, you have outdone yourself as always."

"Don't butter me, Alistair. We both know Ainsley makes superb tea, compared to mine."

"No, Mary, this is quite good."

"Well, thank you," she replied, taking a sip of her own. "Oh, it did turn out well."

They both laughed. "How have you been?" he asked her, again.

She shrugged. "Well, at times. I have done away with my studies for good, though I find myself tempted to resume my work." She pointed to the knitted coasters for the tea. "To resist, I have taken up knitting."

"You did these?" Alistair asked, sliding one close to him to study its pattern and colors.

"No, the lady who teaches me did, but I hope to make some. Perhaps if you're lucky, I will knit you a set of coasters for Christmas."

Alistair smiled at her. "As long as it's not a knitted sweater, I will welcome it into my house."

Mary laughed. "Oh, Alistair, it is truly good to have you here. I've not had this sort of peace in some time," she said, pausing, and he knew what was coming. "Did you speak with Victor?"

Alistair set his tea down and reclined into his seat. "I saw him last night."

"And?"

"And, he says, this is your problem and that he wishes to have no part of it. He is off on his own adventure."

Mary let out a disappointed sigh. "I'm not shocked by his decision, but I was hoping he would be interested."

"No, he has a new hobby."

"The man and his hobbies—to hell with him, Alistair."

"Mary?" Alistair looked to her, deeply concerned by her manner. She was known to be rough and rigid—he knew this too well—but this...this was something darker.

"Forgive me."

He shook his head. "Nothing to forgive. I am here for you."

"I know," she replied, placing her own teacup down. "I found him, Alistair, but I don't know what to do. I cannot sit idle too long because I'm worried his behavior will worsen again, and he'll kill."

"Tell me about him, Mary."

"You know."

"I know he is your brother, and he was in a mental institution. That is not much to go by."

Mary sighed. "He was a devil-child. Our parents despised him, and that is why he was sent away. I did not understand. I pitied him." She looked to the window, seeing her own reflection. "I became a doctor to help him, Alistair. He was doing so well. I convinced them to release him into my custody, promising he would stay here. But then, it happened."

She stopped her story, wiping her tears, but Alistair reached out, taking hold of her hands and comforting her. With a dry swallow, she continued: "He killed Winthrop—my butler. He killed Winthrop and he ran away. It has taken me so long to track him, but I have found him."

"Has he killed since?"

"I do not know, but I do not believe so."

"Perhaps there is a reason, Mary."

"Oh, Alistair, there is," she replied, a cold tone crept up her throat, "he is a monster, and he must be dealt as one."

"Mary, he is your brother. He should be re-institutionalized."

"No, Alistair, even in the institution, he may hurt someone, and I must see that does not happen," she said. "Will you help me?"

Alistair looked into her eyes. They were filled with helplessness. She needed someone—she needed him. "Yes, if it must be done, then I will assist you."

"Thank you, Alistair," she replied, drying her tears with a napkin. "If you would excuse me, I no longer appear proper, and I have grown quite tired."

"I understand, you carry a heavy burden. When you wish to pursue action, you know how to reach me."

"Alistair, you always were the best," she said, kissing him on the cheek.

She turned and went her own way, while the new butler escorted Alistair to the door. He stood on the front-step and took a deep inhale. He had his story, now he needed one for his father.

Chapter V

A Glimmer of Hope

"And that's how it happened," the man said. "Mr. Crumpet?"

"Yes, that is quite interesting, I will run it by our editor," Alistair replied, scribbling down some notes. "If there's nothing else, you may go."

"Thank you, Mr. Crumpet. You have a wonderful day!"

"And you." Alistair looked down at his notes. *William Everhart.* He had written the man's name and nothing else. "This is hopeless."

"Alistair, how's the story coming along?"

He looked up to find Ainsley, joining him at the café. He gave her a puzzled look. "What are you doing here?"

She smiled back. "Is it a crime to have tea?"

"No, but I wish it were. Then, I would have a story to write."

"Oh, Alistair, you've come up with nothing?"

He slid the notebook over. "I've tried doing as father asked, but it's quite difficult. Poor, Mr. Everhart, I fell asleep during his story but promised to tell father." He sighed and sipped the tea he had, but he cringed as it had gone terribly cold. "Enough about me, how did your interviews go?"

"Excellent, father will be pleased."

"You could write about a pigeon in the park and father would be pleased."

"Alistair," she replied, rolling her eyes.

"I'm sorry, that was in poor taste. What does your evening look like?"

"Well, I am going to finish this tea, run back to the *Crumpet*, and then probably go home to Tabby," she replied. "And you?"

Alistair sat back, staring at his notebook. He needed a story, and he needed one badly. "This," he said, pointing at the notebook, "and when I've finished, I may write a spare copy just to burn in the fireplace."

Ainsley smirked. "You need someone, Alistair."

"Ah, is this the pot calling the kettle?"

"No, Alistair, I'm serious. I don't see you out and about, ever. A woman would do you good."

"Ainsley, please," he replied, becoming terribly uncomfortable. "I have friends."

"You do?"

"Well, yes, Victor and Mary and Arthur."

"Arthur is more of an acquaintance, Alistair, and as for Victor and Mary, Victor is odd, and Mary is bad company."

Alistair laughed. "You are right about all three, but at least my closest friend is not my cat."

"What is wrong with Tabby? She doesn't tell my secrets to anyone or get me in trouble."

"No, she just makes messes and stares into your eyes, wishing to steal your soul."

Ainsley laughed, trying to swallow her tea and not snort.

"Alistair, I cannot put up with you anymore," she said, still smiling. She finished her tea and rose up. "I am sorry to run, but I do want to drop these off at the *Crumpet.*"

"It's fine, I wouldn't want to hold you up from your dinner date with Tabby, anyway. What's on the menu tonight, salmon or filet mignon?"

Ainsley gathered her things. "Well, if you come by, you may find out."

"Oh, is this my invitation to make a new friend?"

"Only if you are not busy running around with Victor or Mary. Of course, you'll have to finish father's story first, before you make plans with anyone."

Alistair chuckled at her quip. "Well, save me a plate because it may be a while."

"I will be expecting you then. Goodbye, Alistair."

"Goodbye, Ainsley."

Alistair's eyes returned to his notebook. *What if I make up a story? I could embellish a really good one*, he thought. He began to scribble a few ideas but shook his head. *What am I to do?*

As Alistair stared down, a figure swept pass him and sat across. "Hello, Alistair."

"Victor, what are you doing here?"

"I have good news," he replied, smiling, "I need you tonight."

"Not tonight, I have plans."

"You do?" Victor asked, surprised. "Here I thought you had no one, save me and Arthur."

"Victor, it will have to wait."

"No, it can't!" Victor exclaimed. Everyone around glanced at him, but he leaned forward, whispering, "I made a mistake."

"No—not you?"

"Yes, but it is a good error. Last night was not the last full moon of the month. Tonight is. We have another shot, quite literally."

Alistair's shoulders crashed, as his face sank. "Victor, I have too much. Can this not wait? My father wants a story—"

"And that's what I'm giving you, Alistair!"

"A real story, Victor. One that does not involve—as he put it—*the next London terror*."

Victor sat back and smirked. "This is your big plan0? To find some second-hand story for your father's paper. Alistair—"

"Please, Victor."

"No, this is important. We are doing something for the greater good. Remember, what you do in the light is how you want people to perceive you, but in the dark, that is what defines your character, that is the real you. You are a writer in the light, but what will you be in the dark?"

Alistair chuckled. "The world is not so easily painted in black and white; it has its shades of gray and there is much of that."

"Where do you stand, Alistair?"

"I'm with you, old man, but not tonight."

Victor sighed, shaking his head disappointedly. "I understand, and if you find the time for me, I'd appreciate it."

"Do not be childish."

"I'm not," Victor replied, rising from his seat. "A darkness is coming, though, Alistair, and you best choose what role you are going to play against it. Good luck with the story."

Chapter VI

Changing of the Guard

Alistair walked the cobblestone brick-way, back to the *Crumpet's* office. He had pieced together a story, using William Everhart as the central protagonist; but there was still a weight. He could not tell if it was the story, or if it was his heart's discontent.

Nonetheless, he made his way up the *Crumpet's* stairwell and to the office. There was still a light on. *Father's not left yet*, he thought, filled with a slight worry.

"Hello, father."

The old man raised his eyes, seeming to grumble something under his breathe. "What is it Alistair?"

"I did as you asked," Alistair said, placing the story on his father's desk. "Would you look it over?"

Old man Crumpet slid the paper in front of him, glancing over it. A smile painted his face. There was hope, perhaps Alistair had struck gold. "What garbage is this?"

Alistair sunk into the chair, across from his father. "It's the big scoop you wanted. I tried."

"I wouldn't use this to wipe with, Alistair." The old man sighed heavily, and Alistair knew something was bothering his father.

"What happened?"

Old man Crumpet's jaw tightened, becoming rigid like some statue. "It's your sister."

"What about her?"

"This came in the mail for her." The old man placed an unopened letter on the desk, addressed to Ainsley from *Skyline*.

Alistair looked at it, debating whether to tell his father what Ainsley had told him, but he thought it was best not to. "This means nothing."

"It means enough," the old man replied, pulling the letter back to him, "it means my dream is over."

"We know what your dream is, and it is not over."

"It is," the old man replied, "she's going to join them. My best writer is going to my competition.

"I'll always be here, father."

"God bless you, Alistair, but you can't write a good story to save your life." Old man Crumpet stared at his son. His eyes were full of sadness, but a smirk took his lips. "But you have tall tales, Alistair, and we're going to need them. Bring me one in the morning."

Alistair bolted upright; his eyes beamed at his father's approval. "You're giving me your blessing?"

"Damn my blessing! You two have always done what you wanted. It's time that I back your dream, as you have helped with mine. The *Crumpet's* successful because of your sister and you."

Alistair rose to his feet and swiped his horrid story off his father's desk. "I won't disappoint you."

"I know, Alistair. Now go burn that article on Everhart and get to work on London's next terror."

Chapter VII

This Shade of Grey

"Lager, Ernie," Alistair said, walking by the counter, and straight for his usual booth. Victor already sat there, staring down a glass of scotch. "Cheer up, old man."

Victor sat back and smirked.

Alistair sat down. He waited for Victor to say something witty, but nothing came. In fact, they both sat in silence, with Victor staring at Alistair and Alistair feeling awkward, until Ernie brought the lager.

"I knew you couldn't stay away."

"Oh, are we speaking, now?" Alistair asked, sipping his drink.

"What changed your mind?"

"Nothing," Alistair replied, "my father had a change of heart, so I am here, where I should be."

Victor mused, momentarily. "I wonder, if it was the letter."

"What letter?"

"The one from *Skyline*."

Alistair smiled, dumbfounded. "That was you?"

Victor shrugged. "I needed you here, not there."

Alistair wished to be angry, but he couldn't be. He wanted to be here, with Victor; he wanted to be hunting the werewolf, not another boring story. "You were right, Victor, and I am sorry.

We have roles in this story, and I know which I wish to play in the dark."

Victor chuckled, turning his glass and watching his drink swirl around. "My head is swimming in a sea of scotch, but my mind is still clear. You were right, too, Alistair. The world has its shades, but I must say, this shade of grey does look fitting."

The two men toasted and took a drink. This was how it was supposed to be, drinking, fellowshipping, sharing prudent advice, and hunting London's next terror.

"We do not have much time, Alistair."

"Why not?"

"Our hunter is on the move."

"Where?"

"Across the street. He followed you here."

Alistair stole a glance outside, terrified. "He followed me?"

"Yes, which means none of his actions are random, each is calculated and intentional."

"What do we do?"

"We may not have to do anything."

Alistair did not understand, but Victor knew exactly what was happening. The man across the street ruffled his clothes, and then started for the pub. He was meaning to enter, and Victor knew confrontation was inevitable.

"He is coming here. Is he coming after us?"

"Who else, Alistair?" Victor asked, readying his pistol. "What I don't understand is why. He cannot transform yet, which means he is vulnerable."

"Can he transform on command?"

Victor snickered. "Now, that would be quite the trick."

The fellow entered the pub. He seemed to take a couple deep sniffs. Victor understood. The two locked eyes, and the man approached their table.

"May I sit?"

Victor grinned, goading the fellow. "Everything's better with a drink, friend."

The man reached down, swiping Victor's scotch, and downing it. "May I sit?"

Victor gave a nod. "Next to him."

Hesitantly, Alistair slid over and allowed the man to sit next to him. He did not know what to say, but he kept both hands on his pint of lager.

"Why are you hunting me?" the man asked.

"Why are you hunting us, is the better question?" Victor replied. "After all, you followed us to the docks, correct?"

The man glared hard. "I do not need you complicating things for me."

"And I don't need you killing every Englishmen you come across in wolf form."

"You don't understand."

"I don't?"

The man grunted. "I go to the docks, so that when I transform, I don't hurt anyone, outside of fish sales."

"And last night's outburst was an accident?"

"You followed me."

"I was only doing it for the story," Alistair mumbled out.

The man looked at him confused. "Please, don't speak unless spoken to, Alistair," Victor replied. "As for you, why are you here?"

"I'm warning you. I want to be left alone."

"And I'm trying to purge this city of killers, like you."

"I will not explain again," the man sighed. "Leave me—"

Alistair found himself propping the man back up. It was not close to midnight. Could the man transform on command? Was he?

"Help him to his feet, Alistair," Victor said, rising to his feet. "Ernie, our friend had too much, may we put him in the back?"

"Victor?" Alistair asked, confused. He looked down and noticed the tranquilizer dart, and everything made sense.

"Sure thing, boys," Ernie replied, letting them take the man to a back room.

"Victor, what are we doing?" Alistair asked, as they dragged the man to the room.

"Solving our problem. Be quiet."

When they reached the back room, Alistair found a metal chair, bolted to the ground, and chains. They placed the man in the chair, and Victor began wrapping the chains around him.

"Ernie is well aware," Victor said, noticing Alistair's unsure look.

"Victor, I don't understand? I thought we were going to kill him."

"Kill? Goodness, no. I want to study him, and keep him off the streets," Victor replied. "If you wrote that we were going to kill him in your story, then here's a great plot twist for your readers."

"You're going to study him?"

"Of course," Victor replied, "and when he wakes in an hour, it will be midnight, and he will transform, and we will witness it—firsthand."

Alistair sat down in an empty chair. Ernie walked in, handing another scotch to Victor, who cheerfully took it and sat down next to Alistair.

"This is how it should always be, Alistair. You and I taking care of London's terrors."

"This is not what I imagined, when you gave that speech about us and our actions in the dark."

Victor gave a dry smirk. "As I said, Alistair, I am flattered by this shade of grey."

Alistair stared at the unconscious fellow. "What is your plan with him?"

"I told you, I plan to study."

"But afterwards, Victor? You cannot keep a man locked away forever."

"Why not? No one will miss him."

"You don't know that to be true."

"Alistair, don't start growing a conscious now," Victor replied, rolling his eyes. "I don't care what you do. Have a drink, stay seated, pace, but be quiet and wait with me."

Alistair sighed. He could not drink; if he did, he would be sick. His blood felt thick and heavy, racing through his veins; a chill ran down his spine; and his stomach tied itself up. None of this seemed right.

Chapter VIII

Clementine

When Alistair woke, he found himself on a sofa, covered in a white linen blanket. His eyes glanced about. He was in a messy apartment with clothes strewn out and about and food left lying around. He slowly sat up, and found he was not alone.

"Hello, Alistair, I do apologize for the mess, but Victor gave me little notice," a fellow said, sipping on some tea.

"It's good to see you, Arthur. Working on a story?"

Arthur smirked and looked down at the paper. "Not sure what it is right now, but it's still blank."

Alistair rose from the sofa, shuffled across the room, and sat down next to Arthur. "All good stories begin with blank paper. That's the beauty of it, they can go anywhere the mind wishes."

"Yes, I heard you have quite the tale, after last night."

Alistair stared hollowly at the floor. "I don't. I don't remember anything, honestly."

"Shall I recant? Victor did tell me quite a bit."

"Go ahead."

"Well, Victor went on about some werewolf—I grew tired of it personally, but what could I say? Anyhow, he went on and on about the werewolf, and then, he began to tell me things the werewolf babbled about."

Alistair gave an intrigued look. "Babbled? Werewolves don't

speak our tongue, what did he mean by babble?"

"This one was somewhere between wolf-mind and human-mind—I think it had to do with that tranquilizer. The beast was going on about some woman, though."

"Who is she? What is her importance?"

"I don't know, Victor never said. The wolf just went on about the woman and the end days," Arthur replied, leaning forward and lowering his voice. "I think the end days are near, Alistair, and you have no business getting caught up in the chaos."

Alistair gave a dry swallow, studying Arthur. They were very much alike—storytellers with wide-open imaginations—but Alistair stared a little longer and noticed Arthur's sadness and regret. Yes, this white-haired fellow was nearing his own end days; he had lived a full life; and Alistair understood Arthur wished the same fortune for him as well.

"I appreciate your advice, Arthur, but I am already trapped in this story."

Arthur chuckled. "The spider never catches the fly, Alistair, it's the web."

"What if this story is different? What if the fly catches the spider?"

"I've never heard of such a tale, but for your sake, I hope you are right." Arthur rose from his seat, pocketing the blank page, and glancing at his pocket watch. "I have business to attend to. Victor should be back soon."

"Where'd he go?"

"To find the woman," Arthur replied, "best of luck, little fly."

Alistair watched as Arthur left the apartment. *He's right,* Alistair thought, *I am merely a fly battling an unseen spider in this shade of grey.* He let out a sigh and strolled to the window side.

All those little people with important lives. What would they do, if the end days were indeed near? Alistair gave a dry swallow and whispered:

> Stuck by the windowpane,
> I watch the streets below;
> Bustling to and fro,
> where do the people go?
> The sky is always gray
> and the rain falls gently,
> But I'm happy in this state,
> this state of feeling empty.
>
> Hanging on my crumbling walls,
> there's worn out photographs,
> And glancing to my bedside,
> there sit my dreams of glass.
> If I lit this scene on fire,
> would all burn to ash?
> But it's hard to leave this prism trap,
> when it's all I have.

"Well put," Victor's cold voice said.

Alistair turned away, finding his friend and a strange woman in the room. She wore a dark green dress, reminding Alistair of a woodland; her hair was a fiery orange, hopefully not indicating her behavior; and she had rich, enchanting honeycomb-colored eyes.

"I did not hear you come in."

"You did not hear anything last night, either," Victor replied, seeming to condemn Alistair for falling asleep at the pub. "Introductions are in order. Ms. Clementine, this is Alistair Crumpet, and, Alistair, this is Ms. Clementine."

"A pleasure to meet you," Alistair said.

"Likewise," Clementine replied. Her voice was stern, and Alistair guessed she knew of Victor's doings.

"Well, let's all have a seat, and we will discuss what we know," Victor said, ushering Ms. Clementine to the couch.

When they each had a seat, Victor began, "Now, I believe—"

"Where is he?" Ms. Clementine asked.

Victor gave a perplexed look. "In a safe place, in safe hands, nothing will happen to him. I wish to study him, and—"

"I don't care what you want, you are vile," she replied, turning her attention to Alistair. "You helped him?"

"I am, uh, I am a sort of assistant, but I did not know his plan."

"Alistair!"

"I did not know your plan, I'm not going to lie to her, for your account."

"Enough," she snapped. "I don't care who did it, but you will release him."

"I cannot."

"You will, and you better hope the packs have not heard about it."

"Packs?" Alistair asked.

"Yes, werewolves travel in packs, just as any other canine," she replied. "Worse for you, is the fact that I have a relationship with this one, and I will call for my sister-covens to help intervene."

"That would be quite the story, right, Alistair?"

"Victor, I think she is being honest."

"I am too. Imagine a bunch of witches flying down here on brooms. Would be a fantastic piece in the *Crumpet*."

"Mr. Victor, who should I give you to?" Ms. Clementine asked, aloud. "Should you go to Lillia Wren? Perhaps Lindon Flint would be better at torturing you? No, I should send you straight to Hell with Elessia Oates."

Victor grinned. "My dear, if you plan on throwing names out, at lease make sure I know who they are."

"You don't now, but you will, if you do not release the werewolf you have."

"Why would a werewolf mean so much to a witch?" Victor asked. "Let's deduce. Now, covens would only intervene for two reasons. The first being, that he is of royalty, but we know that is not true—he's a lone wolf. That leaves only one other reason, he has an intimate relation with a witch—possibly even you—

and the covens will do anything to keep him safe." Victor's smile widened. "Which is it, my dear?"

Ms. Clementine returned a hard glare and cunning smile of her own. "You think you are clever, but you know nothing beyond your own realm," she replied. "He is the one born of wolf and magic, he is the heir of the Wolf-King, and the one promised to save us from the end days—hence my being here."

Victor's smile dissipated, as Alistair sat on the edge of his seat. "What is coming, Ms. Clementine?" Alistair asked.

She looked to Alistair and spoke, "Something stronger than all of us, save God. It is coming to bring the end days, and only Thane can save us."

"Now the wolf-man has a name," Victor chided. "Why should we believe his coming is a sign of the end days? What proof is there of it?"

"I am here," she replied. "There will be three attempts to end the world, and this is the first. The sign has always been when the son hunts for his mother—that was prophesied at his birth—and the time is now."

"Who is his mother?"

"I am."

Victor and Alistair sat quietly, as their bodies stiffened at the revelation. "You are the wolf's mother?" Victor asked.

"The Wolf-King's mate?" Alistair added.

"Yes, and I will not ask for his release again. Either you do it, or I will have you both hunted down and killed."

"Victor will release him," Alistair said.

"What? I am studying him."

"Victor will release him," Alistair said, again. "Ms. Clementine, what is coming? What is he saving us from?"

Ms. Clementine smiled, eyeing them both. "You will see, for you have added yourselves to this story."

Chapter IX

He Who Knows Most

It was five minutes until seven. Alistair had missed dinner with Ainsley once, and he would not dare try it again. It was not his fault; Victor had dragged him into another adventure, but Ainsley would not understand. She never seemed to, though she acted as if she did.

Alistair knocked on the door and waited. It opened, and there she was. Her muddy eyes stared at him, patiently waiting for an excuse on his missing dinner the night before. But he could only smile.

"You are a sight for sore eyes, Alistair," she said, finally breaking the tension.

"I'm here for dinner."

"That was last night," she replied. She seemed irritated by this, but her eyes shifted to the room behind her. "You're timing is impeccable, little brother."

This transpiring confused Alistair, but Ainsley moved aside, and he understood, deeply regretting his decision to arrive for dinner. On the sofa, there sat a fellow—a fellow many disliked, save old man Crumpet.

"Mr. Shooler, I did not know my sister was playing host."

Mr. Shooler smiled. "Yes, well, I invited myself since I was hungry for something delicious."

Alistair stepped into Ainsley's apartment. Immediately, the smell of seasoned lemon sauce filled his nose, and he knew she had been preparing chicken.

"Hello, Tabby," he said, petting the cat as she rubbed her head against his pantleg.

"Yes, quite the grimalkin, isn't she?" Mr. Shooler asked.

"Grimalkin? I'd say otherwise."

Mr. Shooler laughed at the response. "Oh, Alistair, you are quite the ultracrepidarian. Grimalkin means a domestic house cat."

Alistair braced himself, knowing he'd been insulted. "And ultracrepidarian?"

"Ah, you are merely a fellow who speaks beyond his own scope of knowledge."

Alistair cringed, but Mr. Shooler took no notice, as he sipped his glass of wine. "Dear Ainsley, would you fill my glass again?"

"Of course, Mr. Shooler."

Alistair took a seat on a chair across from Mr. Shooler. He could see into the kitchen, and Ainsley shot him a painstaking face. They were both in for a long dinner.

"Ainsley, where did you disappear to?"

"I'm coming," she replied, returning to the sofa side, and filling Mr. Shooler's glass.

Mr. Shooler's eyes glanced from the filled glass, to Ainsley, and he exhaled cravingly. "You are indeed a bellibone, my dear."

"Belly bone?" Alistair asked.

"Wine, Alistair?" Ainsley asked, not wishing to dwell on Mr. Shooler's awkward flattery.

Alistair took an empty glass from Ainsley, and she filled it for him. After she had topped off her own glass, she took a seat on the sofa—very much edging herself away from Mr. Shooler and his end.

"I have enjoyed your news of late, Ainsley. I'm surprised *Skyline* has not offered you a position."

"You are too kind, Mr. Shooler."

"No, no, the credit is due," he replied, leaning near her. "If you are ever in need of a splatherdab, I will gladly assist."

Ainsley smiled dumbly, not knowing what to say. "Alistair deserves far more credit than I."

Mr. Shooler eyed him, snidely. "I'm surprised you have never written about a case of boanthropy."

Alistair raised his glass to his lips. "I'm not familiar with the case."

Mr. Shooler grinned. "When I was a journalist, we had to be familiar with such terms, and be an expert of our craft. Sadly, your father seems to publish anyone."

Alistair choked on his sip of wine, but Ainsley resolved the situation quickly. "I believe the chicken is ready. We will be having beans and sautéed onions, too," she said, rising from her seat, and leading the way to the table.

Ainsley prepared the plates, while Mr. Shooler lathered his

roll in butter, and Alistair brooded over his half-empty glass of wine.

"It all looks delectable, my dear," Mr. Shooler said, salivating over his plate of food. "Now, what shall we talk about? I must warn you both, I am quite the deipnsophist."

"What?" Alistair asked.

"What of bardolatry?" Mr. Shooler asked, ignoring Alistair. "I am quite the Shakespeare fanatic."

"I do adore *Romeo and Juliet,*" Ainsley said.

"*Hamlet* for me," Alistair chimed in.

"Rubbish," Mr. Shooler replied, "*Taming of the Shrew.* It displays much wit, and puts women in their rightful place, serving men."

"I don't believe that was the moral," Alistair said, recollecting the tale. "It is more about choice and equality."

"Ah, Alistair, you are showing your ultracrepidarian ways again."

"Mr. Shooler, I do not wish to end dinner so abruptly, but Alistair and I must work on a story."

"Do not let my presence bother you. I may be able to help with your story—after all, I am quite the splatherdab, my dear."

"Mr. Shooler, I would have you splather and dab in our story, if I could; but alas, this story is secret."

"Oh, a juicy bit?" Mr. Shooler drooled at the thought of the gossipy piece. "Could I have some edgy details?"

"I am afraid not, but I will offer you first read."

"Fair enough, dear Ainsley, I am quite gambrinous, anyway."

Mr. Shooler rose from his seat, and Ainsley escorted him to the door. Alistair did not bother to follow, but he strained his ear, eavesdropping, only to hear more awkward flattery by Mr. Shooler. Then, the door shut.

Ainsley returned to the table; her face was flushed of all color. "I despise his haughty ways."

"Yes, he is quite the crêpehanger, who believes he is a soigné fellow, but is nothing more than a spermologer and stalko."

Ainsley stared, smiling proudly. "That was quite a mouthful, little brother."

"Yes, well, I have been holding it all night," Alistair replied, and he and Ainsley broke out into laughter.

Chapter X

Ordog

"But Death has snatched you, with its whispering tune, taking your beauty, and leaving us one wonder, too few."

The actor stood tall, elevating his arm upward, and applauses resonated through the theatre. The play was over, and the curtains were drawn back, while the actors and actresses scurried onto the stage for one last bow.

Alistair had seen the play many times. It was a rendition of the Greek lovers, Orpheus and Eurydice, yet in this play, the lovers were named Ruric and Belinda. Just as Eurydice in the Greek tragedy, Belinda passed away, and Ruric entered the underworld to ask for her return. The Master of Underworld granted Ruric's request, under the condition that he not look back on Belinda, until reaching the mortal world. But just as Orpheus, Ruric failed, looking back shortly before exiting the underworld; and he lost his love forever.

"Well, that was long," Victor complained. He shuffled, uncomfortably, in his seat; he had been known to be a lover of tragedies and comedies, but his nerves were on edge tonight.

"It was well done," Alistair replied.

"Well done or not, we have business," Victor said. "Where is that witch? I have not seen her all night. Do you think it's a trap?"

Alistair shook his head. "No, I trust her."

"You trust her?"

"Of course. We gave her what she wanted."

"That's the problem, we gave her our only bargaining piece in all this."

The two ceased talking. The actors and actresses returned backstage, while everyone started filing out of the theatre. The two continued waiting.

Alistair took out a pen and pad, jotting down some notes. He knew the ushers would be coming around to force people out, but they would leave him alone, knowing who he was and believing he was critiquing the play. Victor sat beside him, unhappy.

"I need to light one, Alistair."

"Not now. You know you can't in here, and if you go out, they won't let you back in."

Victor groaned. His hand went for the silver cigar case in his vest. He was tempted.

"Gentlemen," a voice said.

"Ms. Clementine," Alistair replied, rising to his feet to greet her, while Victor rolled his eyes.

"Are you both ready?" she asked.

"We've done this before," Victor replied. He glanced to Thane. "After all, we caught him."

"You shot me at a parley," Thane growled.

"Enough," Clementine said to him. She looked to Victor and

continued, "It will be different this time. I told you."

"And I listened. You said something of your wolf-boy and the end of the world. What I fail to understand is, how do we fit in?"

Clementine smiled. "And I told you, you injected yourself into this story. He is coming, though."

"Who?" Victor asked.

"One of the Great Ones," Clementine replied, "he has come to end the world, but it is prophesied that he will fall to the one born of wolf and magic. There is only one, and that is Thane."

"How do you know? What if there's another half-breed?"

"There is no one else, and there will be no other. It is now forbidden for races of the enchanted world to marry someone outside of their people."

"Why?" Alistair asked. Clementine's words captivated him, teaching him more of a world he knew existed, but knew nothing of.

"It has always been forbidden, but the prophesy of wolf and magic has always existed. The Wolf-King, Temptus, sought to tear down the barrier, he asked for my hand, and I gave it to him. In the end, it cost him his life, as he was butchered by an unknown shadow. Thane is the only born of wolf and magic."

"When we first spoke, you said that there would be three attempts to end the world. Are there prophesies for the other two?"

Clementine never answered Alistair, as the lights to the theatre went out. They each stiffened, straining to hear anything unusual. Then, an eerie red glow came from the stage, and a low grey smoke slowly swept across it, drawing their attention.

"If you want to wolf-out, now is the time," Victor whispered, as he rose to his feet, and took hold of his pistol.

"It doesn't work like that," Thane replied.

"How convenient."

"What is happening, Ms. Clementine?" Alistair asked.

"He's coming."

"Who?"

"Ordog."

The sweet sound of a reed pipe filled the theatre.

"We need help," Thane said to Clementine.

"There is only us."

Thane growled and turned to Victor. "Shoot me."

"What?"

"Shoot me. I cannot control my changing, like other wolves, I can only turn on a full moon, or if I am hurt."

"Well, why didn't you say so," Victor replied, raising his pistol, and shooting Thane in the chest.

Thane fell back, wincing with pain. Blood trickled from his wound. He spoke truthfully, though. His eyes shifted—the animal was coming—and his body writhed with pleasure and pain, as it transformed. Clementine placed her hand on his head, whispering a charm, and placing him under her control.

Then, a figure appeared on the stage. A satyr, with the torso of a man and the lower body of a goat with black cloven hooves. The reed pipe ceased, as the satyr gave a crafty grin towards Alistair and company.

"Welcome, to my hellish abode."

"This is not your home, or your world," Clementine replied, drawing her wand from her satchel.

"My dear, every stage is mine, for I am the protagonist, while your Lord above is my antagonist."

"If that is so, then we have your deuteragonist," Victor chimed in. While Alistair was terrified, Victor's scotch had clearly given him a false confidence.

Ordog's grin widened. "Born of wolf and magic, but truly accepted by neither. I have no fear."

As the last words fell from Ordog's forked tongue, a fiery whip appeared, and the satyr slung it out towards Thane. Clementine raised her wand, casting a spell to shield them all from the whip's grasp, and Thane attacked.

Ordog's flaming whip disappeared, as the satyr's figure morphed into a mighty demon. The demon reached out, grabbing Thane by the throat and slinging the wolf-man to the ground. Thane jumped back up, snapping at the demon, but Ordog took hold of him and beat him viciously.

"Victor, do something!" Alistair shouted, realizing Thane was dying.

Victor raised his pistol, but from the stage, the fiery whip appeared again, and it snapped out, knocking Victor off his feet, and rendering him unconscious.

Clementine raised her wand, casting a shield again, protecting herself and the two men from the whip. "Alistair, we need your help."

Alistair stooped down, picking up Victor's pistol. The feel of the gun metal reminded him of how he despised such weapons. Nonetheless, he took aim at the demon, though his hand shook.

"Alistair!"

Alistair fired, hitting the demon in the chest. Ordog looked out and grinned—who was this mortal to challenge him? He tossed Thane aside and started for Clementine and Alistair.

Clementine raised her wand in the air, making a sweeping motion with it. Alistair could feel it. A strange force was pulling him towards her, and it grew stronger and stronger.

"Your powers cannot match mine," Ordog goaded.

Clementine did not answer him. Alistair reached her side, holding onto her satchel, while propping Victor up.

"Your God will deny you!"

Clementine gave the demon a cold glare. "He will, but I will see that He is the one who ends this world, for He is the Alpha and Omega."

Ordog growled. "You are a witch; you are one of mine."

"I serve no one. I am I."

Thane's body flew off the stage, passing Ordog, who howled in anger; and once she touched Thane, they disappeared.

Chapter XI

In God's Cathedral

"Forgive us our trespassers," Alistair mumbled. What were the rest of the words? He never was good at remembering the prayer. Of course, he never aligned himself, or saw himself, as a religious fellow.

"Mr. Crumpet, I did not expect to see you here."

Dazed, Alistair looked up. "Mr. Snipes, hello. Please, sit with me."

"Well, thank you, kindly," Mr. Snipes said, taking a seat. "From our last conversation, I did not take you for a man of faith. Have you found it?"

Alistair gave a wry smile. "I don't know what I've found, Mr. Snipes. I'm adapt to seeing monsters and horrors, but something has happened of late, which has shaken my faith, and I have come to seek some higher answer."

"Mr. Crumpet, we are friends, so please, call me James—or better yet, Jimmy." Mr. Snipes bowed his head and made a crucifix. "Amen," he whispered. "Now, my dear Mr. Crumpet, I know how you feel, for I have seen my own horrors."

Alistair smirked. *Blessed are the eyes of the lamb.* "My pardon, Jimmy, but I'm afraid you have never seen anything like this."

"Sin is sin, is it not?"

"I do not speak of sin, Jimmy."

There was a moment of silence between the two. "When I was in Africa, during my tour, I committed my share of heinous sins. We would go from village to village, raping women, killing men, and selling children." He looked to Alistair, whose mouth sat slightly agape. "Oh, yes, Mr. Crumpet, I partook in those deeds." He raised his hand into view. "Then, the accident happened during a raid, and I was placed in a hospital, and that's where my outlook changed."

"What happened?"

"Well, I lay there dying in my own piss and shit." Jimmy crossed himself and whispered: "Forgive me Father." Then, the old man continued: "I realized my life was being wasted away. To my superiors, I was just another number that was easily replaceable, but I also realized I was just another number from this world's view. I was nothing. I was no better than the men beside me, and I was no better than the men who died before me."

Alistair nodded his head. "A sobering moment."

Jimmy grinned. "You are right with that point, Mr. Crumpet. I prayed that if there was a God—a higher being or power—I prayed that I might be spared, so that I could turn my life around. I wanted to be better, and I still wish to be."

"I think you have attained that, Jimmy. You have a good heart, you speak with truth and wisdom, and you come here, praying and seeking God."

Jimmy chuckled, shaking his head. "All that, that is nothing. It makes a difference in my life, but not one on the world. The real battle is not in these four walls, Mr. Crumpet; the real battle is out there, in the world. I'm not talking about the good Christian battle; I am speaking of the battles man inflicts upon man, brother against brother. When we all learn to love, we will know the good Lord's plan, but until then, we will continue falling short."

"You discredit yourself, Jimmy. You make a difference. Already, we have spoken twice, and you have uplifted my spirits and returned my faith that not all things are dire."

"Well, that's a kind thing to say, Mr. Crumpet. What problem do you face?"

Alistair sighed. "Do you believe in other worlds, which coexist with ours?"

"Well, that depends. I believe in some of the occult. I have seen a medicine man pull someone from near death, with only an insect."

"There are other worlds, Jimmy. I have seen them, and you and London have read about them. Something new has come, though; something I could never imagine," Alistair replied, staring to the crucifix of Christ, which sat aloft on the wall. "Something has come to end the world. I thought I was prepared, but I was terribly wrong. I'm drowning, Jimmy; I'm drowning in a sea of black. A void has come to swallow us all, and I have seen it."

The two sat silently. The choir continued singing their hymns, while nuns walked about, comforting those in the chapel. Jimmy looked to Alistair.

"You may feel lost, Mr. Crumpet, but remember, the good Lord never gives us more than we can handle."

"Do you believe that?"

"Does it matter?"

The reply caught Alistair by surprise. "I don't know what to believe anymore."

"My pardon, Mr. Crumpet, but you do," Jimmy replied, "you believe in what you see. Whatever horror you saw has you rattled, and now, you feel you misplaced your faith. You are back peddling, Mr. Crumpet, you are attempting to place your faith in religion, but that has never been you."

"You are right. I have always placed it in friendship and writing."

"Why has that changed? The good Lord will watch over you, for He is the Shepherd, and we are His flock. He gives us what we need to face trials and tribulations, and for you, He has supplied friendship and words." Jimmy rose from his seat. "If I were you, Mr. Crumpet, I'd get busy."

"And you will feel the fire again, if Ordog is able to end the world."

"I thought there would be three attempts," Alistair said.

"There may be three, but Thane needs us, if we wish to escape this first one."

"What plan do you have?" Victor asked. "Last night, we went in blindly, and we had no chance of challenging your demon."

"Ordog will stay at the theatre. He loves the irony, that he is the master of the stage, and we all must watch, as he destroys our world."

"I would be ending the world, now. Why doesn't he leave?" Victor asked.

"Because a spider never leaves its web," Arthur answered.

Clementine nodded. "Thane is still loose. I will go and confront Ordog, but I need you and Mr. Alistair to escort Thane to the theatre and give him a chance to end Ordog."

Victor looked to Alistair, who nodded in approval. "All right, we will help you one last time."

Clementine cast a few charms and spells, restoring Thane to full health, and waking him. She told him of the plan, and he agreed with it.

The four left the apartment. It was a grey day, muggy and rainy. When they reached outside, they found a buggy waiting for them, with Mr. Snipes at the reins.

"This is my piece in your story, Mr. Crumpet," he said, smiling down at him.

They boarded the buggy. Oddly enough, Mr. Snipes' presence did

something to their moods; it strengthened them. Here, this old fello
clearly knew the danger, but he had come to them, ready to help.

The buggy jostled down the streets, straightway for the theatre. N
words were spoken; none needed to be said. The rain drizzled on th
outside, as the gloomy buildings loomed over their travel.

Then, the theatre came into sight. A place, which was supposed t
harbor laughter, tears, and joy, sat naked, hollow, and glum. It wa
as if the theatre knew this was its final act.

"I will go in the front; you three should go in the back."

"We should stay together," Alistair replied.

Clementine shook her head. "Do as I say."

No one else argued. Victor, Alistair, and Thane walked around t
the back of the theatre, finding an unlocked door. They quietly darte
through the dark halls, making their way passed empty dressin
rooms and racks of costumes.

"How will you kill Ordog?" Alistair asked Thane.

"He cannot be killed, but if I can give him a mortal wound, then he
will be unable to enter our world again."

"What do you want us to do?"

Thane strained his ears, hearing a fiery whip crack, and magica
charms block and parry. "Enter from the left side of the stage, quietly
and open fire on him. I will save you."

"Save us?" Victor questioned, but Thane vanished, leaving Victor
and Alistair.

"Well, here goes nothing," Alistair muttered.

The two men dashed out. They found Ordog wielding his fiery

About the Author

Originally from Columbus, Ohio, Dakota McElhinny also spent time growing up in Morganton, North Carolina. Between the two, he gained the 'bustling city life' and 'rural country life' experience. After receiving his Associate of Arts degree from Western Piedmont Community College, he obtained his Bachelor of Science from North Greenville University. Currently, Dakota lives in South Carolina, working as a ghostwriter, editor, and book author.

To this date, *Crumpet Court Chronicles* is Dakota's eighth self-published book. *The Realm* (2016), *The Realm: Rise of the Demon Prince* (2017), and *The Realm: The Chess Master's Ring* (2020) make up his epic fantasy *The Realm* series. *Time Frozen Mirrors* (2018), *Black October* (2019), and *Dreams of Glass* (2020) are his three poetry books with *Time Frozen Mirrors* featuring poems "Let My Love" and "Box Full of Wishes" and *Dreams of Glass* featuring "Beyond One Step". *The Art of Time* (2020) is his stand-alone short story compilation.

For all questions and inquiries, Dakota can be reached at: dakotawrites100@gmail.com

Epic Fantasy Series by Dakota:

Book I: The Realm
Book II: The Realm: Rise of the Demon Prince
Book III: The Realm: The Chess Master's Ring

Poetry Books by Dakota

ime Frozen Mirrors   Black October   Dreams of Glass

Short Story Book by Dakota

The Art of Time